Cat-astrophe at the Opera

Lee Aucoin, *Creative Director*
Jamey Acosta, *Senior Editor*
Heidi Fiedler, *Editor*
Produced and designed by
Denise Ryan & Associates
Illustration © Chantal Stewart
Rachelle Cracchiolo, *Publisher*

Teacher Created Materials
5301 Oceanus Drive
Huntington Beach, CA 92649-1030
http://www.tcmpub.com
Paperback: ISBN: 978-1-4333-5597-4
Library Binding: ISBN: 978-1-4807-1719-0
© 2014 Teacher Created Materials

Written by
Janeen Brian

Illustrated by
Chantal Stewart

Contents

Chapter One

Such Singing, Such Music

Silhouette, Minuette, and Eugene had always wanted to go to the Paris Opera.

Silhouette gave a deep purr. "Such singing," she said. "Such music."

Minuette's voice tinkled. "*Oui*, Silhouette! I agree."

"Me, too!" bellowed Eugene. The other cats promptly clapped their paws over their ears.

"Softer, Eugene, please," said Silhouette.

"You'll need to be much quieter when we go to the opera," scolded Minuette.

"Being quiet isn't fun," sighed Eugene.

Silhouette stroked her whiskers. "We need money to buy tickets for the opera," she said.

"*Oui*," said Minuette. "And we have none."

"Couldn't we sing for money?" asked Silhouette. "Others do."

Minuette loved the idea. "Oh, *oui, oui*!"

"Can I sing, too?" asked Eugene. Minuette and Silhouette looked at each other.

Silhouette took a deep breath. "Yes, of course, Eugene. You're our friend."

Chapter Two

A Fine Day for the Opera

It was a fine, warm day. The three cats stood on the wide steps of the opera building.

Silhouette wiped her paws. Her heart thudded. "Ready?" she said.

"*Oui,*" said Minuette. "You start, Silhouette."

Silhouette began to sing. Her song was soft and warm like a summer morning. Several people stopped and dropped coins in their bowl.

"*Merci,*" said Silhouette. "Your turn now, Minuette."

Minuette's voice rippled like a small stream. The friends received more coins.

"*Merci,*" said Minuette. "Now you, Eugene."

Eugene took a deep breath and let out a song that sounded like a screech of pain. People hurried by with their hands over their ears. No one gave any coins.

"Please, Eugene, stop!" cried Silhouette. But Eugene didn't hear her.

Soon, a man dropped ten coins into the bowl. "Now, stop that awful noise!" he shouted.

Eugene gulped. His whiskers drooped. His eyes filled up.

"Come on," said Minuette, patting his shoulder. "It's all right. We have enough money. We can go inside now."

13

Chapter Three

Magnifique!

As the three cats stepped into the opera house, they gasped. Tall lamps lit up a large, swirling staircase. Sparkling chandeliers hung from decorated ceilings.

15

"It's beautiful," said Silhouette.

"*Oui*," said Minuette. "*Magnifique!*"

"I'd love to sing here," bellowed Eugene, looking around. Silhouette hurried to the ticket office.

"Sorry, the tickets are sold out," the ticket seller said.

"But we have the money," cried Silhouette. "What can we do?"

The ticket seller leaned close. "Come with me," she whispered. "You can stand in the wings at the side of the stage." The cats' eyes widened with excitement.

"*Merci!*" said Minuette to the ticket seller. "We'll be very quiet." She tried not to look at Eugene as she said it.

Carefully, they peeked through a gap in the huge, red curtains. "Oh!" they meowed together.

In front of them were hundreds of people. They sat in long rows or in one of the golden balconies. Minuette almost toppled backward when she looked up at the painted ceiling. The columns and statues made it seem like a palace.

Just then, a conductor tapped his baton. He raised it. The orchestra began. The opera, *Madame Butterfly*, was beginning. Silhouette's fur stood on end.

"It's starting!" whispered Minuette as the great curtains suddenly swung open.

Hours passed. The cats' eyes glistened as they watched the actors. Their tails and whiskers moved with the music. Their hearts pounded. But none of them uttered a sound.

Chapter Four

Encore!

Finally, near the end, Eugene whispered, "Let's climb to the top of the curtains to get a better view."

"We can't!" hissed Silhouette.

"*Non*, Eugene, *non!*"

"But we'll see much more from up high," said Eugene. "Please. We're not doing any harm!"

"All right," Silhouette finally agreed.

Paw by paw, they crept to the top of the curtain edge. Then, to their horror, the music stopped. People were clapping. The opera was over.

"Hang on!" Silhouette squeaked as the great curtains swished closed.

When they finally stopped, Silhouette, Minuette, and Eugene were left clinging to the curtains. Wild-eyed, they faced the audience. A lady pointed and laughed. Soon, everyone was pointing and laughing.

"Sing, little opera cats, sing!" someone called.

"We have to go!" cried Silhouette, alarmed. One by one, they scrambled down the curtains and onto the stage.

"Sing!" rose the chant. "Sing! Sing!"

Silhouette and Minuette rubbed their paws in fear.

"Sing! Sing!"

Silhouette knew they had to do it. She sang her song, and then Minuette sang hers.

The audience cheered.

"Now, we really have to go," whispered Silhouette. But Eugene had stepped up to the front of the stage.

"Oh, no," murmured Silhouette.

25

Eugene opened his mouth. But to his friends' amazement, his voice didn't screech or wail. It boomed. It reached the tall ceiling and the golden balconies. It was a big voice. And it had found a big space in which to sing.

Eugene finished his song and bowed. His two friends clapped along with everyone else. "Wonderful, Eugene!" they said.

The audience thought so, too. "*Encore!*" they cried. "*Encore!*"

Finally, Silhouette, Minuette, and Eugene sang one last song together.

They would never forget their day at the Paris Opera.